Now I Know
the Story of
Samson

Written by
Jan Allen

Illustrations by
Russ Allen

www.lightbugspublishing.com

NOW I KNOW THE STORY OF SAMSON

Published by Light Bugs Publishing, 3749 D. Gulf Breeze Parkway, Suite 336, Gulf Breeze, Florida 32563.
Printed in China.

All Scripture quotations are taken from The King James Version of the Bible (KJV).

Library of Congress Control Number: 2005938176

ISBN: 0-9765514-1-1

This book is dedicated to…

My Lord and Savior, Jesus Christ
My parents, Dennis and Jan Allen
Jaime Scott
Jake and Elizabeth Rembert
Dr. Stan and Kristin Lewis
Dr. Ted Traylor
Dr. Dean Register
and
Larry Mott

Hey, kids! It's me, Sally, and I'm going to tell you a story about a real-life superhero.

I'm not talking about one of those make-believe superheroes who climbs and flies between 50-story buildings. This superhero really lived—just like you! He lived a long time ago, back in Bible times, in a land called Israel.

JUDGES 13-16

SAMSON

This superhero was super, super, super strong. He fought thousands of bad guys all at one time and he won! He even wrestled a lion and won. Fighting was something this superhero knew all about.

Yep, he had big arms and a big chest like all muscle men. But, he also had a really BIG heart. It was a big heart for God!

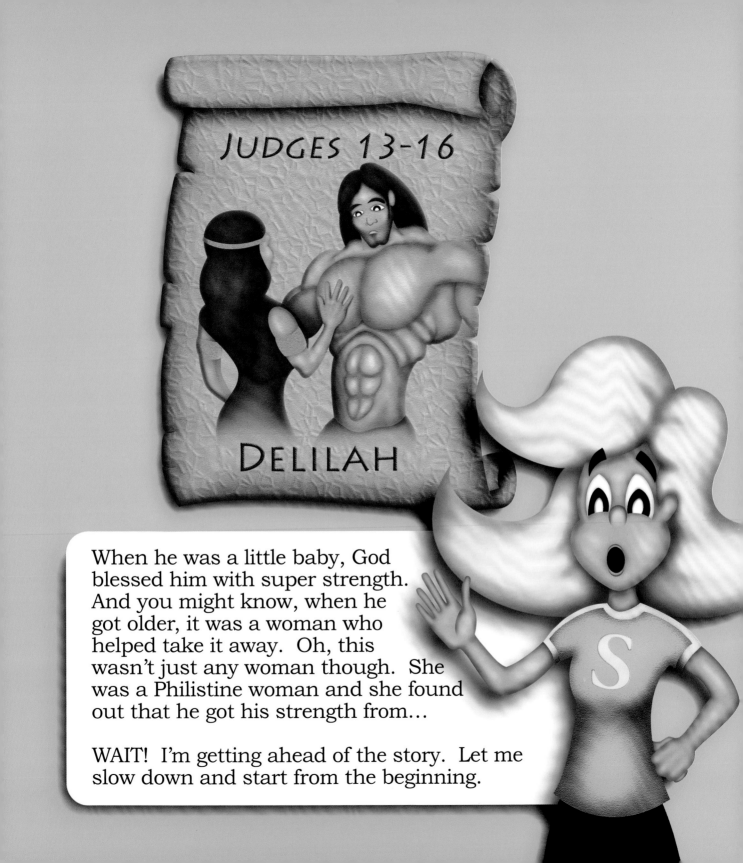

JUDGES 13-16

DELILAH

When he was a little baby, God blessed him with super strength. And you might know, when he got older, it was a woman who helped take it away. Oh, this wasn't just any woman though. She was a Philistine woman and she found out that he got his strength from...

WAIT! I'm getting ahead of the story. Let me slow down and start from the beginning.

This story starts with the good guys from Israel called the Israelites and the bad guys from Philistia called the Philistines. The Israelites were God's special chosen people. And, um...uh...let's just say, the Philistines were not God's special chosen people.

The Israelites were terrified of the Philistines and for good reason. Those Philistines were a mean and cruel bunch. There were so many of them. And, they had great weapons too. Well, they had great weapons for Bible times. So, eventually, they took over and started ruling the Israelites. For forty years, the poor Israelites were beaten and bullied and treated just awful.

So, what does this superhero have to do with all of this? Just hold on, I'm getting to that. Telling a story takes time, you know.

Judges 13:1

One day an angel of God came down and visited an Israelite man and his wife. The angel told them they were going to have a baby boy. Since they didn't have any children, they were overjoyed.

The angel said the boy was going to be a special servant of God, called a Nazirite, and he would begin to rescue the Israelites from the Philistines. Then, the angel told them something else. He said the boy's hair could never be cut. Never, never, never, ever. Wow!

Well, anyway, just as quick as he came, the angel left in a flame of fire.

So, the baby was born as the angel had said; and, the happy couple named him Clyde.

Judges 13:3-20

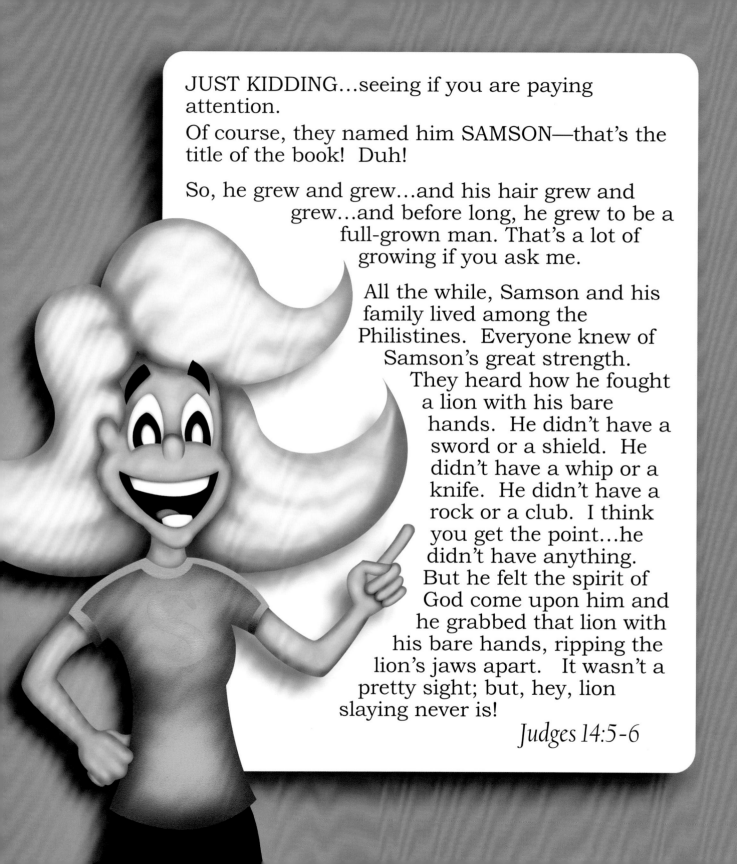

JUST KIDDING...seeing if you are paying attention.

Of course, they named him SAMSON—that's the title of the book! Duh!

So, he grew and grew...and his hair grew and grew...and before long, he grew to be a full-grown man. That's a lot of growing if you ask me.

All the while, Samson and his family lived among the Philistines. Everyone knew of Samson's great strength. They heard how he fought a lion with his bare hands. He didn't have a sword or a shield. He didn't have a whip or a knife. He didn't have a rock or a club. I think you get the point...he didn't have anything. But he felt the spirit of God come upon him and he grabbed that lion with his bare hands, ripping the lion's jaws apart. It wasn't a pretty sight; but, hey, lion slaying never is!

Judges 14:5-6

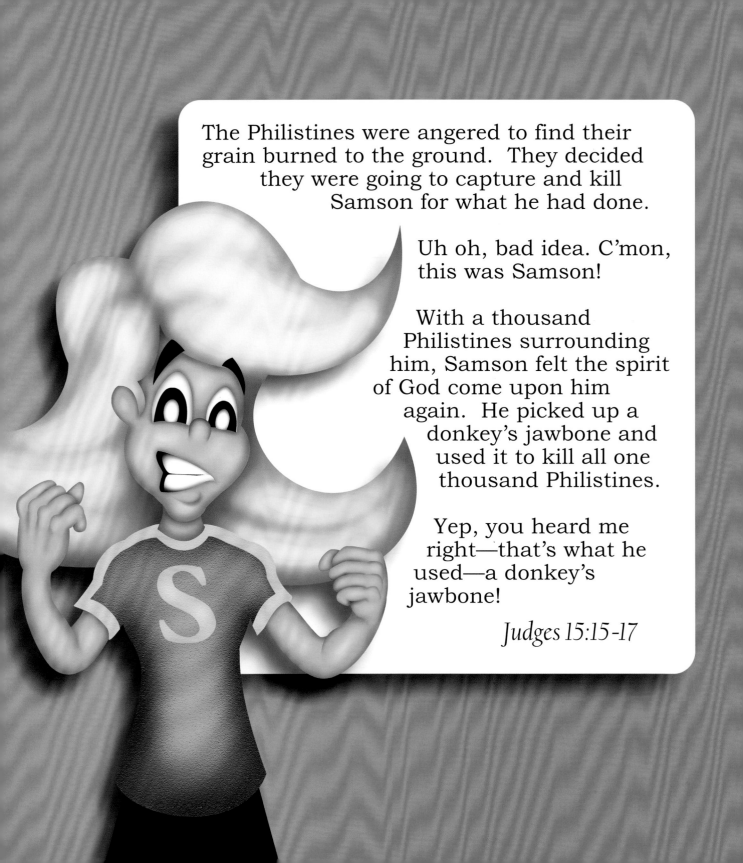

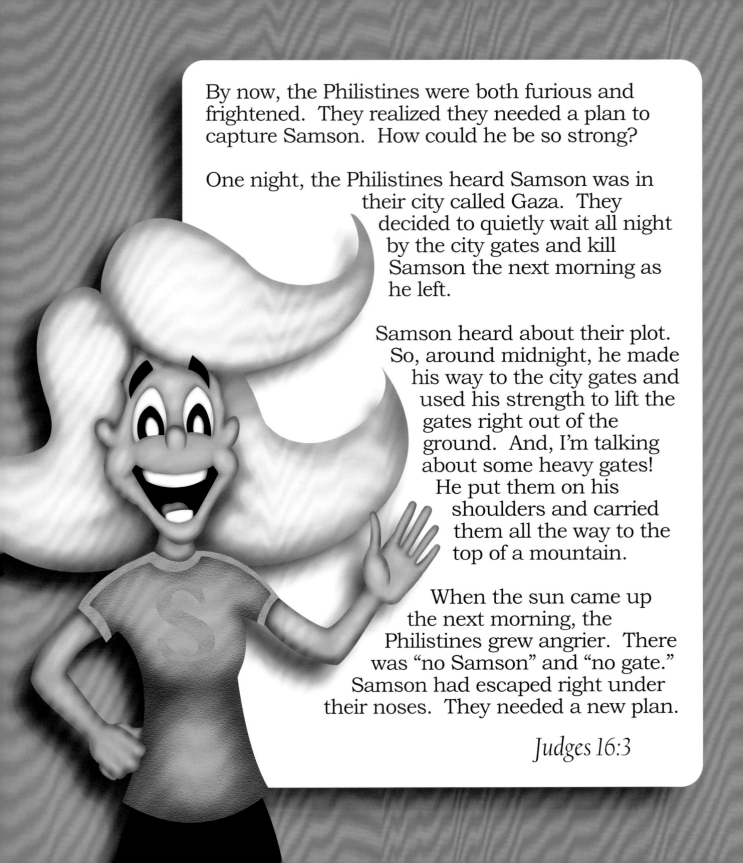

By now, the Philistines were both furious and frightened. They realized they needed a plan to capture Samson. How could he be so strong?

One night, the Philistines heard Samson was in their city called Gaza. They decided to quietly wait all night by the city gates and kill Samson the next morning as he left.

Samson heard about their plot. So, around midnight, he made his way to the city gates and used his strength to lift the gates right out of the ground. And, I'm talking about some heavy gates! He put them on his shoulders and carried them all the way to the top of a mountain.

When the sun came up the next morning, the Philistines grew angrier. There was "no Samson" and "no gate." Samson had escaped right under their noses. They needed a new plan.

Judges 16:3

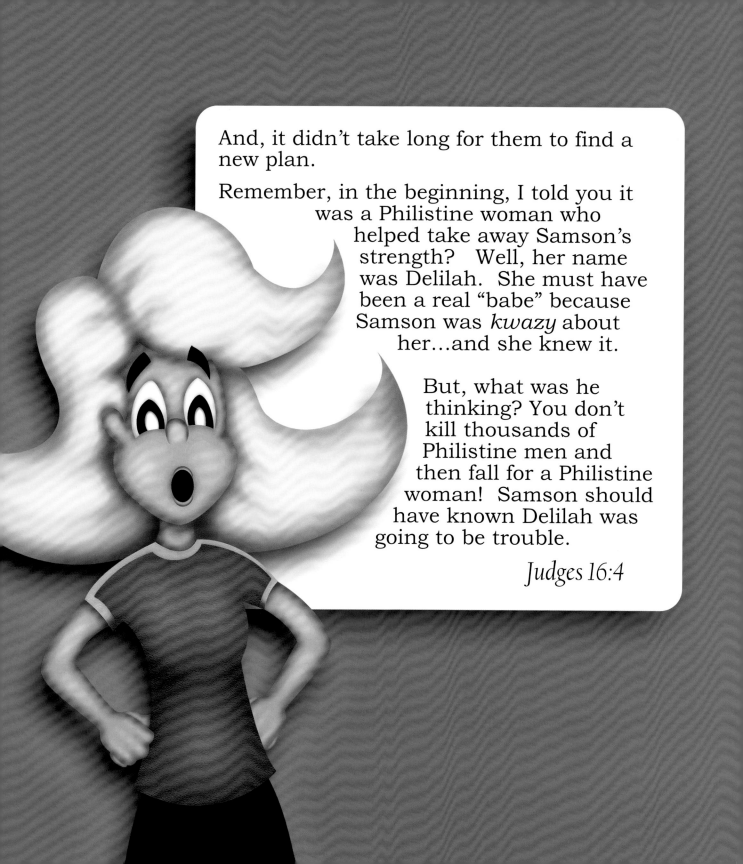

And, it didn't take long for them to find a new plan.

Remember, in the beginning, I told you it was a Philistine woman who helped take away Samson's strength? Well, her name was Delilah. She must have been a real "babe" because Samson was *kwazy* about her...and she knew it.

But, what was he thinking? You don't kill thousands of Philistine men and then fall for a Philistine woman! Samson should have known Delilah was going to be trouble.

Judges 16:4

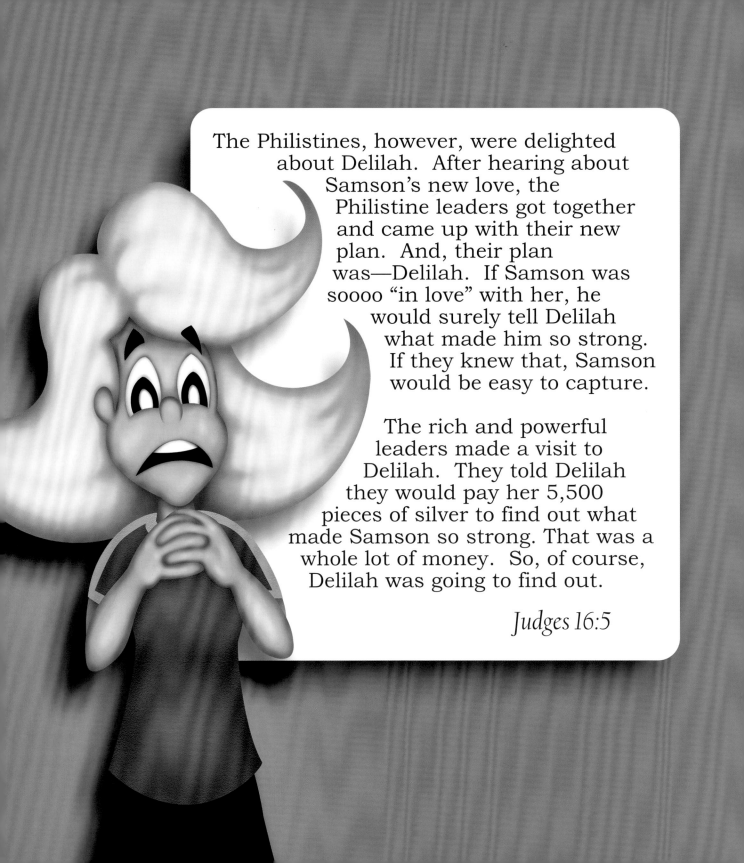

The Philistines, however, were delighted about Delilah. After hearing about Samson's new love, the Philistine leaders got together and came up with their new plan. And, their plan was—Delilah. If Samson was soooo "in love" with her, he would surely tell Delilah what made him so strong. If they knew that, Samson would be easy to capture.

The rich and powerful leaders made a visit to Delilah. They told Delilah they would pay her 5,500 pieces of silver to find out what made Samson so strong. That was a whole lot of money. So, of course, Delilah was going to find out.

Judges 16:5

Like I said, big, strong Samson was bonkers over Delilah. She was sure she could find out the secret of his strength.

Delilah began to beg Samson to tell her what made him so strong. Not wanting to give away his secret, he told Delilah if he were tied with seven raw-leather bowstrings, he would surely lose his strength.

Don't you know Delilah was excited to hear his secret. She was probably getting ready to count her money.

Judges 16:6-7

So, the Philistines brought Delilah seven raw-leather bowstrings. While Samson slept, Delilah tied him up. Then, she yelled that the Philistines were coming. Samson jumped up and easily broke the bowstrings. Delilah was annoyed and, again, she begged Samson for the reason he was so strong. This time, he replied that if he were tied with new rope, he would definitely lose his strength.

So, the Philistines brought a new rope. As Samson slept, Delilah tied him with the rope and yelled that the Philistines were coming. Samson jumped up and snapped the rope. Delilah didn't like it that he had lied to her and she pleaded for the real reason he was so strong. Samson told her that if she were to weave his hair into her loom, he would absolutely lose his strength.

So, while he slept, Delilah used her loom to weave Samson's hair and yelled that the Philistines were coming. Samson woke up and yanked his hair away. Delilah began to whine to Samson saying that if he loved her, he would tell her the truth about his strength. Every day she whined until her whining finally paid off. Samson told her the real truth—he was a Nazirite and if his hair were ever cut, he would be as weak as everyone else.

Delilah realized this was the truth. She immediately sent for the Philistine leaders who brought their barber and cut off Samson's long hair. Yikes! Once again, Delilah yelled that the Philistines were coming. Samson tried to jump up, not realizing that the Lord had left him. His hair and his super strength were gone. Samson was helpless as the Philistines took him away. He had trusted Delilah and she had tricked him.

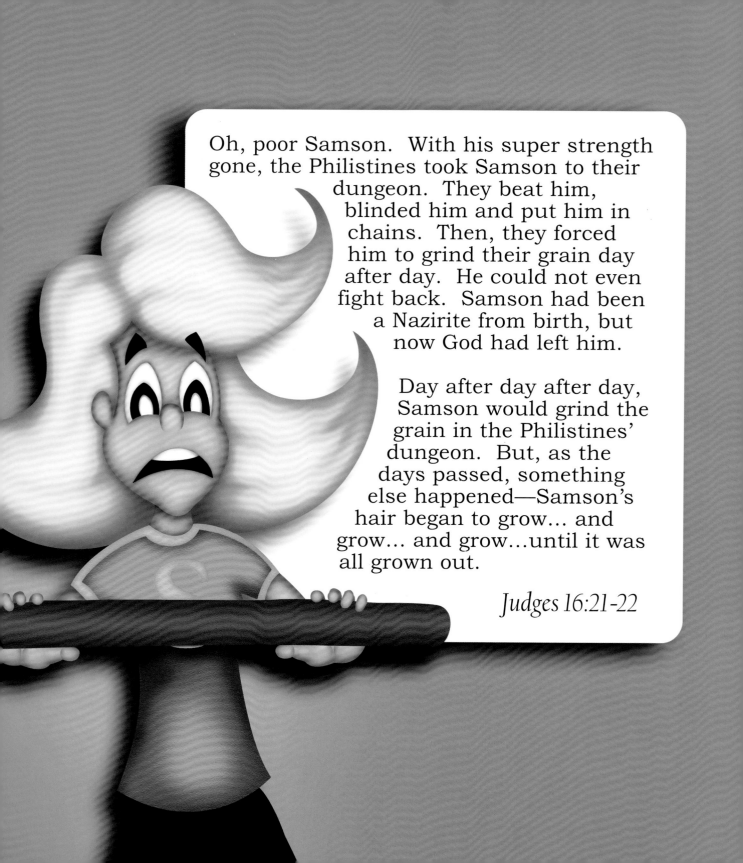

Oh, poor Samson. With his super strength gone, the Philistines took Samson to their dungeon. They beat him, blinded him and put him in chains. Then, they forced him to grind their grain day after day. He could not even fight back. Samson had been a Nazirite from birth, but now God had left him.

Day after day after day, Samson would grind the grain in the Philistines' dungeon. But, as the days passed, something else happened—Samson's hair began to grow... and grow... and grow...until it was all grown out.

Judges 16:21-22

Naturally, the Philistine leaders were excited about capturing Samson and decided to celebrate. The Philistines' celebration took place in the temple where they worshiped their idols. The leaders thought it would be fun to bring Samson out of the dungeon so everyone could make fun of him.

A young boy led Samson to the center of the temple between two big pillars that held up the roof. Samson asked the boy to help him place his hands against the pillars so he could rest on them. So the boy placed Samson's hands on the pillars.

It was quite a celebration. The temple was full that day and the excited Philistines were having a great time laughing and making fun of Samson. Until…

Judges 13:23-27

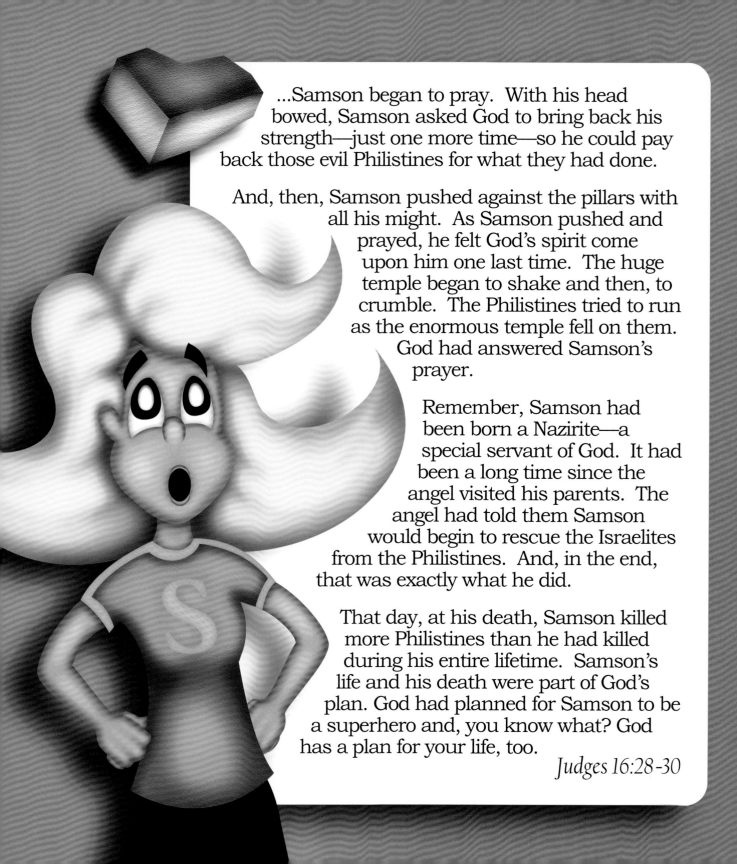

...Samson began to pray. With his head bowed, Samson asked God to bring back his strength—just one more time—so he could pay back those evil Philistines for what they had done.

And, then, Samson pushed against the pillars with all his might. As Samson pushed and prayed, he felt God's spirit come upon him one last time. The huge temple began to shake and then, to crumble. The Philistines tried to run as the enormous temple fell on them. God had answered Samson's prayer.

Remember, Samson had been born a Nazirite—a special servant of God. It had been a long time since the angel visited his parents. The angel had told them Samson would begin to rescue the Israelites from the Philistines. And, in the end, that was exactly what he did.

That day, at his death, Samson killed more Philistines than he had killed during his entire lifetime. Samson's life and his death were part of God's plan. God had planned for Samson to be a superhero and, you know what? God has a plan for your life, too.

Judges 16:28-30

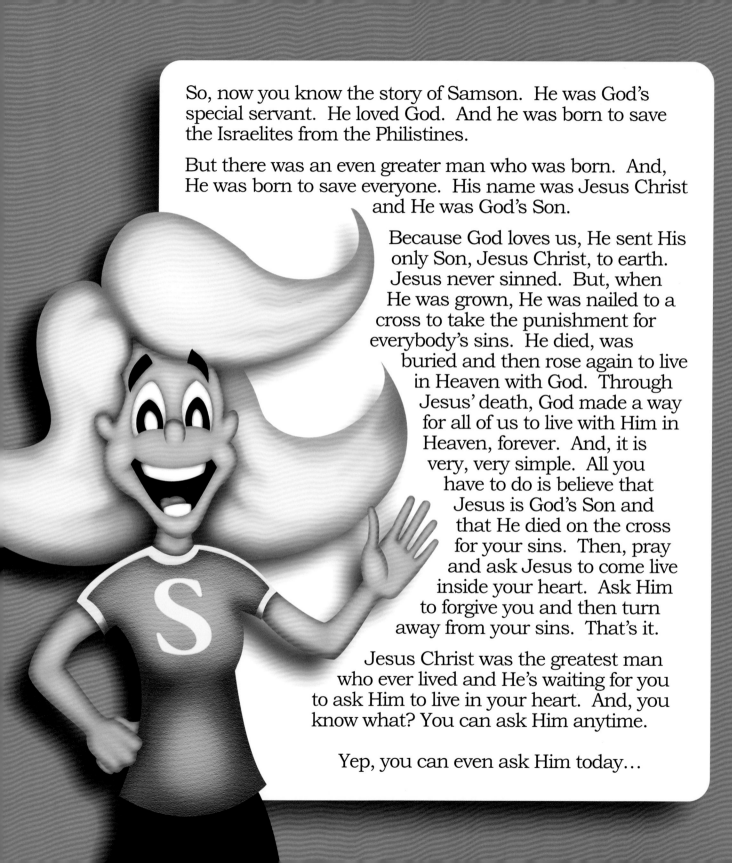

So, now you know the story of Samson. He was God's special servant. He loved God. And he was born to save the Israelites from the Philistines.

But there was an even greater man who was born. And, He was born to save everyone. His name was Jesus Christ and He was God's Son.

Because God loves us, He sent His only Son, Jesus Christ, to earth. Jesus never sinned. But, when He was grown, He was nailed to a cross to take the punishment for everybody's sins. He died, was buried and then rose again to live in Heaven with God. Through Jesus' death, God made a way for all of us to live with Him in Heaven, forever. And, it is very, very simple. All you have to do is believe that Jesus is God's Son and that He died on the cross for your sins. Then, pray and ask Jesus to come live inside your heart. Ask Him to forgive you and then turn away from your sins. That's it.

Jesus Christ was the greatest man who ever lived and He's waiting for you to ask Him to live in your heart. And, you know what? You can ask Him anytime.

Yep, you can even ask Him today...

For God so loved the world, that He gave His only begotten
Son, that whosoever believeth in Him should not perish,
but have everlasting life. John 3:16

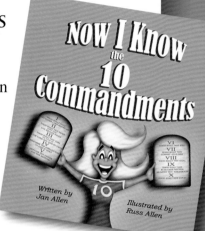
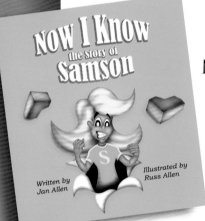
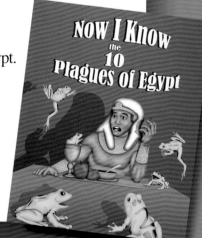